All The Things We Saved You From

Amy Laurens

Other Works

SANCTUARY
Where Shadows Rise
Through Roads Between
When Worlds Collide
The Complete Sanctuary
    Series

KADITEOS
How Not To Acquire A
    Castle

SHARDS OF FATE
Touchstone

STORM FOXES
A Fox Of Storms And
    Starlight
A Stag Of Snow And Memory

SHORTER WORKS
All The Things We Saved
    You From
Bones Of The Sea
Christmas Miracle Is Just A
    Saying
Dreaming Of Forests
Rush Job
The Ice Cream Crown
    Skating Races
Trust Issues

COLLECTIONS
And Then I Shall Transform
April Showers
Change Becomes Us
Darkness And Good
For A Little While
It All Changes Now
Of Sea Foam And Blood
The Inklet Collection
Where Your Treasure Is

NON-FICTION
How To Plan A Pinterest-
    Worthy Party
On The Origin Of
    Paranormal Species
The 32 Worst Mistakes
    People Make About Dogs

INKPRINT WRITERS
How To Write Dogs
How To Theme
How To Create Cultures
How To Create Life
How To Map

Find other works by the author at
www.amylaurens.com/books

All the Things We Saved You From

Amy Laurens

AUSTRALIA

Print ISBN: 978-1-922434-95-1
eBook ISBN: 9798224006892

www.inkprintpress.com

National Library of Australia Cataloguing-in-Publication Data
Laurens, Amy 1985—
All The Things We Saved You From
60 p.   cm.
ISBN: 978-1-922434-95-1
Inkprint Press, Canberra, Australia
1. Fiction—Fantasy—Contemporary 2. Fiction—Fairy Tales, Folk Tales, Legends & Mythology

Summary: Trapped by fae exploiting his magical ability to turn sunlight into gold, Tristan must decide the price he's willing to pay for his freedom.

First Edition: June 2024

Cover design © Inkprint Press
Cover image © Mystic Quill Creations
Raven image © Corsiva via Pixabay

For Sophie (Year 8/2016), for reasons she will
never remember.

Also Nicole (10/2022). I hope you find your
revenge.

All The Things We Saved You From

To the casual observer, the light was spectacular, a golden evening glow that bathed the glassy skyscraper in the middle of nowhere and set its windows aglimmer as the sun sank toward the horizon and the world held its breath.

Ravens circled somewhere about the building's knees, full and luscious oaks a gilded fringe at the building's toes, autumn-gold leaves fairly dripping with the evening light.

Exactly the right sort of clouds filled the sky, tiny cumulonimbuses that might have been painted in with a fairy's brush, all cotton candy-pink and dewdrop-gold as the last of the daylight flared magnificently.

Still air bore the pleasant scent of leaf mould and lake water, for the skyscraper stood alone in the middle of the woods, held up by magic and willpower only in a place that usually bore no love for mechanised things.

No trace of concrete dust in the back of the throat here, no hum of traffic or lingering scent of fuel winding about one's neck like a scarf, or a boa constrictor. Instead, birds chirped and cawed and warbled, leaves rustled secretively, and the occasional trout broke the mirrored lake with a tiny splash, breeching the sacred surface of its world to snag an unwary mosquito.

It was all very beautiful—and for Tristan, it was all very pointless. Here was a man who, once, had been lured to the wood by the promise of beautiful things and, once, had been ensnared by the serpent that lay beneath them.

Once, unfortunately, was enough.

Because instead of golden light glimmering off the gently rippling surface of the lake, instead of the enlivening sting of a bug sucking blood through his skin and the tingling, soul-ringing *slap* that followed, instead of the smell of oak leaves winding down his sinuses like an intoxicating perfume, Tristan lived in the penthouse of the highrise, where the cooling system stripped all flavour from the air, where the golden, gleaming light of sunset filtered in through heavily tinted windows except at certain hours, and where the only noise not of his own making was the energy powering his prison's various appliances.

Tristan was miserable.

Nobody cared.

Sometimes—like now, as he sat on a padded window bench that he suspected had been intended as a cozy nook but instead merely illuminated the fact of his solitude and the utter lack of other people he needed to nook away from—Tristan suspected that he was miserable because he deserved to be.

Perhaps he'd imagined this, a prison of his own mind made real by the magical forces that wreathed and writhed through the forest. Perhaps this was only the tangible form of that which had always been: an impenetrable fortress in his mind, self-selected isolation birthed by the suspicion that, really, what value did he have to anyone as a person anyway?

He'd run away from his father at twelve.

His mother, he'd never known.

He'd wanted her, and she hadn't wanted him, and there began a path that led, without very many twists and turns at all, to the window seat on which he now sat, surveying the kingdom that in his more whimsical moments he thought of fondly as his.

A flock of ravens exploded from a nearby oak, their wings catching the last of the sunlight like a bear dipping its paw in honey.

Tristan shifted restlessly. The thing was—the thing *was*—that in actual fact the prison was entirely of his own conception, because at any moment—any moment at all—he could pick himself up off the padded bench, pad his way barefooted across the thick vermillion rug, and descend the interminably long staircase to the world below.

At least, he could if he could bring himself not to care about two highly important things:

One, the life of his daughter Nicole, and two...

He leaned against the window, the glass cold against his shirt sleeve, against his cheek. Any moment... Any moment now...

The tinting on the windows lifted, and Tristan was bathed in the full strength of the golden sunlight. Warmth suffused him, buoying him up until he bowed backward, full to bursting with the life and light of it all. Pressure built in his chest, mounting, mounting...

Warmth became heat...

Breath became light...

...and as Tristan exhaled, a deep-chested sigh of contented pleasure, the air in front of him condensed, and flakes of gold crystallised therein.

He raised his hands, cupped, and the flakes drifted down as the motion of his exhalation released them.

Half full.

Not the best day, but not the worst.

The sun dipped below the horizon. The tint rose up again on the windows. And Tristan crossed the vermillion rug diagonally to the white marble plinth that most people would have called the kitchen bench, and let the gold flakes fall into the transparent crystal bowl that sat there for that purpose, joining the rest of the week's harvest and sending the numbers on the scales that coastered the bowl flickering.

The numbers settled.

Adrenaline gave Tristan's heart a tweak.

Two kilos. It was enough.

The doorbell rang, and even though the door was never locked—what would be the point, when the only being Tristan cared to keep out could walk on through regardless, and the rest of the tower slept uninhabited—Tristan crossed the rug on the opposite diagonal toward the door, nervous hands wiping against his thighs, leaving sparkling tears down the front of his slacks.

The bell chimed again, and although it was the only noise apart from the background hum of electricity, still there was an element of discordance to it, as though it were clashing painfully with a sound that sat just barely out of hearing.

"I'm coming, I'm coming," Tristan muttered quietly—very quietly. A deep, steeling breath and he yanked the door open—though not too forcefully.

The man-who-was-not-a-man gleamed back at Tristan, not emanating a single photon of light and yet still somehow causing the dim, maroon hallway to brighten to something slightly less... intestinal. Dark hair gleamed as though lit by the sun that had died, tousled as though the wind itself was in love and couldn't help but caress; dark eyes glittered with an eternity of amusement, and ears tapered to slender points that Tristan could never keep his eyes completely away from, though he did, with monumental effort, constrain his fingers from them.

"May I enter?"

He would enter with permission or without, but

it went better for everyone with.

Idly, Tristan ran a thumb over the long scar that tracked down the side of his wrist. "Please," he said in a tone that formed the Venn diagram intersection between loathing, and longing, and desperate, desperate need.

The man-who-was-not-a-man strode over the vermillion rug to the crystal bowl of gold. He lifted it in both hands, the crystal chiming a long, gleaming note of recognition, and inhaled deeply as one might a bowl full of eucalyptus steam to clear the throat. "Yes," he sighed happily. "You have done good work this week."

The gold vanished, and despite his intentions every single week to spot how it was done, Tristan still couldn't decide if the gold had been *inhaled*, or merely vanished.

Sometimes he hoped for vanished.

Most times he hoped for vanished.

To think of the gold as something he'd exhaled and the other had then inhaled...

A shiver slid down his spine, silver and cold.

"You'll make sure Nicole gets her half?" Tristan said, imagining the curved point of that ear beneath his thumb, for him to caress—or crush.

The man-who-was-not nodded, shrugged, lazily tilted his head and narrowed an eye at Tristan. "You still care? Even after all this time?"

Tristan hadn't known a snake still coiled in his gut, but if he had he'd have named the snake Regret. Or maybe Guilt. Sorrow, even; Sorrow was a great name for a snake. "Yes," he said quietly—very quietly. "I still care."

A more decisive nod this time from the man-who-was-not. "Then I shall return again next week."

No one had wanted him in his early life, and too many had wanted him in his middle life, but at least now in this, his imprisoned life, there was a balance: Tristan made something worthwhile, and in exchange, he would not be torn apart—and neither would his daughter.

Nicole scowled deeply as the man-who-was-not-a-man appeared on her living room rug, specifically at the audacious curl of his dark hair over his pointed ears.

The coffee mug in her hands was too hot. She set it down on the scuffed wooden dining table—barely large enough for three—and ran her finger absently over the chip in its navy rim, firmly putting aside the idea of throwing it at him.

The coffee would stain the cream rug, and if the rug was a little threadbare in places, it was still exceptionally clean. She wasn't prepared to jeopardise that, especially not for *him*.

"Careful," he said. "Your face will freeze that way."

The quirk of his lips was meant to be a careless grin, she supposed, but she'd been studying his kind for well over a decade now—unbeknownst to him, of course—and she could smell his unease almost as easily as he smelled it on a human.

He stepped closer regardless, invading her space, his leafy green scent covering her like algae on a pond. Closer, he bent over, lips hovering a mere breath from her cheek as she held herself taught, a bowstring ready to loose, except she couldn't afford to arrow him, not yet, not now, not *here*.

His damp tongue slid up the curve of her jaw. "I could rearrange your face for you if you liked," he breathed.

There was a toothed wolf in her chest, and its name was Fury.

He'd never dared actually *touch* her before.

"In there," Nicole said, pointing with arm outstretched at a large round fishbowl set on the shelf by the front door, framed by trailing pothos and potted heartsease sunning themselves in the slanted square of sunlight slowly tracing its way down the wall.

And if her outflung arm happened to press him away from her, what of it?

With a shrug, he turned on his heel, strode to the fishbowl, and held out his hand over it, palm down. He exhaled on the back of his hand. Breath spiralled out. Gold flakes rained into the bowl, now filled nearly to the brim, glittering hopefully in the sunlight.

"Leave," she commanded.

He hesitated, his back to her, a movement in his shoulders or neck or the tiny sliver of jawline she could see suggesting that he was about to speak—and then he didn't, and he vanished instead.

Nicole exhaled herself. No gold flakes appeared in front of her, but she did receive a satisfying sense of catharsis and relief.

She rolled her neck. It popped.

I'm safe now, she reminded herself. *He'll never touch me again.*

He'd flirted with the line plenty of times before, and today he'd finally crossed it—but that was fine, because she'd known that this was inevitable, and the bowl was full. The trap was laid.

It was time.

IT WAS NOT TIME FOR THE EVENING FLASH YET, THOUGH IT was close enough that Tristan was sitting on the padded bench seat staring out—as usual—at oaks he couldn't smell, lake water he couldn't taste, and ravens he couldn't hear.

There was a knock at the door regardless.

Tristan's brow creased, an origami folding of emotions into a sculpture titled 'Unfamiliar'—for a moment the prize exhibit in Tristan's penthouse apartment that was otherwise titled 'Consistency'.

The knock sounded again, a little louder and more urgent this time.

Tristan crossed the vermillion rug, the pile plush under his bare feet, and made it to the cool grey floor tiles beyond.

A third cascade of knocking, hard and fast, a hummingbird's heartbeat.

Tristan yanked open the door, cutting the sound off mid-flow.

A young woman, her face reddened, her mouth set in a hard line, paused in her abuse of the door. Her clothing was uncanny, sweat marks under her arms, her high-waisted jeans something almost like women had worn when he'd been a little younger than her but… thicker? Stiffer? The cut was off somehow, anyway, and her ribbed shirt—sunset orange, he could appreciate the confluence of that with her timing, just moments before sunset—crap, sunset.

He whirled away from the girl, cast a hasty 'Come in' over his shoulder, and hurried back across the island of the rug to the ship of his bench seat, whereon he could at least *feel* like he sailed briefly beyond the confines of his very expensive prison, floating on seas of sunlight as he exhaled them into gold.

She stood on the red rug, no longer a sunset but a tequila sunrise.

"I just need to do something," Tristan said, gesturing vaguely at the window, at the sinking sun.

The air conditioning kicked up a notch, probably in response to the warmer air the girl had brought in with her, and Tristan caught the scent of a fruity, floral sort of perfume.

Definitely a tequila sunrise, and here he was, a... distractedly, he racked his brain for memories of cocktails with the word 'sunset' in them. Surely there had been one.

Also, she was staring at him oddly, and he caught the sense that maybe—just maybe—thirteen years of imprisonment hadn't done wonders for his conversational skills.

The girl shifted her weight on the rug, not nervous, simply reasserting her presence in the room. "I'm Nicole," she said. "Your daughter."

Tristan blinked as something cold cascaded through his chest. "But... you're..." *Old* was definitely not what he meant, but it was the only word on the tip of his tongue, so he choked it back.

Grown? Matured? How exactly did he politely point out that someone he'd last seen in single digits was now obviously an adult in every sense and capacity without seeming rude?

He was staring.

He stopped.

The tint on the windows was still dark, but the sun was dropping inexorably down, its lower rim already hidden by the billowing oaks on the horizon, and the tint would lift very soon, and he couldn't afford not to catch it when it did because he needed the sun, needed the light to spin into gold, needed the gold to give to his captors, to pay them off and to pay for his…

Daughter.

He peeked out of the corner of his eye. She was still staring at him, expression inscrutable.

She didn't *seem* particularly poorly.

"You're… here," he finished lamely. And then, "Why?"

"I didn't come to rescue you," she said scathingly, "if that's what you think."

"No?" he said, shame chasing the surprise. Of course she hadn't. Of course she hadn't. And that was fine, and the sun was sinking so this had to be a brief incursion anyway—or else he could briefly excuse himself from it—but… but… If she *hadn't* come to rescue him, why on earth was she here at all?

"I want you to teach me your trick." Her feet scuffed in the rug, but it wasn't nerves; instead, she seemed almost absent; he didn't know *what* it was.

The surprise returned in full force, gripping his chest so hard he struggled to breathe. He clutched the edge of the padded window bench, the seam pressing against his fingertips. "I'm sorry, what?"

Tristan's chest, which had a moment ago gone cold, now heated nearly to boiling.

His… trick?

His *trick*?

The rare and exceptional skill he had, which had literally caused the death of several people—in a roundabout way, at least, greed was cunning like that and when you had money and were desperate for more, there were ways of ensuring the competition stayed out-competed permanently—the skill that had nearly gotten *him* killed several times, that had cost him his family, his freedom…

His *trick*?!

Half of him was outrageously offended at the belittlement.

The other half needed her to run, screaming if necessary, and never return, because—"You have no idea what you're really asking for."

"Yes," she said, gaze perfectly level, "I do."

The tint on the window lifted. Tristan's shoulder was instantly warm.

He twisted, his back to his daughter—god, how resonant that felt, drawing instantly to mind images of the last time he'd seen her, how he'd had to turn his back on her as she played on the new cream rug he'd bought just for her, so she'd have somewhere clean on the floor to play with her primary-coloured blocks; she loved building, loved construction, loved making things, and he'd turned his back on her and walked away because he'd been told if he didn't, none of them would survive—cold anger at the man-who-was-not flashed through him, a burning desire to take the top of those elf-pointed ears and twist them clean off…

Tristan inhaled deeply as the last sunlight of the day washed over him, its presence as real and as breathtaking as an oceanic wave.

Warmth suffused him, buoying him up until he bowed backward, full to bursting with the life and light of it all. Pressure built in his chest, mounting, mounting…

Warmth became heat…

Breath became light…

…and as Tristan exhaled, a deep-chested sigh of frustration, and resentment, and all sorts of complicated emotions, something golden crystallised in the air in front of him.

He caught it in cupped hands.

It twinkled in the dying light, a cool-toned yellow.

The tint rose on the windows.

Tristan squeezed his eyes shut against the tearing agony that squeezed his chest, because it wasn't gold flakes cupped in his hands, it was pyrite, fool's gold, because he was a fool, and he'd forgotten the first and most important rule: he was only valuable to his captors so long as he was happy, and his family was only safe as long as he was valuable to his captors.

Tristan was miserable.

People only cared if it interfered with his ability to be singularly, blindingly, excruciatingly *happy* for four critical minutes a day.

"Please," he whispered into the dark behind his eyelids. "You have to go. He'll be here soon, and I…"

He swallowed, let his cupped hands fall to his lap. Squeezed fingers shut around worthless flakes of complicated emotion that were nothing like what they wanted.

You must think only of joy, if you want the process to be consistent, the not-a-man had said, that first time in the forest when Tristan had come seeking guidance, seeking fortune—seeking glory. *Never of anything else. That will taint the process and make the results worthless. And we wouldn't want you to be worthless.*

It had been a long time since Tristan had thought of the not-a-man's teeth, almost as pointed as his ears.

Nicole shuffled on the rug, and this time it *was* a nervous shifting. "It... didn't work?"

Tristan shrugged without opening his eyes, offered the contents of his hands up for her presumed inspection.

"Is it... Is it because I'm here?"

Her eyes were wide, and her confidence had dropped away.

He gave her a frown that was meant to be a smile. "No," he said. "Not really." It had been a long time, but he'd been plenty capable of distracting himself, in the early days.

"Then... why?"

He could not tell her. He could look right into her blue-grey eyes, eyes he'd dreamt of for more than a decade, and just... not tell her.

He shifted on the seat, leaning his shoulder against a window that, now the tint had come back up, felt cold. "You have to think only of joy."

Her lips worked at that, pressing and twisting and writhing. "You enjoyed being here, away from us? From... me?"

A surge from that snake in his gut. "No." *But I pretended I was to keep you alive.*

Her mouth writhed some more, but she nodded. "I guess he'll be here soon regardless?" Her shoulders tensed as she awaited the answer.

Tristan nodded.

"What will you do?"

Tristan shrugged. The same thing he'd done all the other times he'd failed, back in the early days, back before he'd learned that in this life, for him, success meant rigid self-control (at least for those four minutes a day). "You'd better go before he arrives," Tristan said, though what he really wanted to say was, 'Stay, see what happens, what it's like, then you'll know why asking me to teach you my *trick* is insanity.'

Nicole turned on the vermillion rug, walked to the door, and left, pulling the door shut behind her.

It was a good thing the window was already holding Tristan up.

Nicole pressed her back against the wall in the corridor and breathed deeply of warm air that was, after the filtered, air-conditioned air of her father's apartment, a little cloying.

A minute or two, she figured, give or take. Tristan—she'd long thought of him such, first out of anger and spite, then out of deliberate emotional distancing, and at last simply out of habit—had seemed quite firm in his desire to get rid of her, though to be fair that could be because of what had happened, rather than what was going to happen.

What *was* going to happen?

She bunched her lips to one side and decided that was still up for dispute.

Pressing her back even more firmly against the wall, she did her best to disappear into the shadow formed by a sort of artistic alcove, and waited.

Only briefly, as it transpired, because a moment later the not-a-man appeared at Tristan's door. Nicole just barely caught her hiss of surprise before it escaped her teeth.

Not-A-Man rang the doorbell, one she could have sworn hadn't been there when she had knocked, though who knew, perhaps she'd just been distracted. The somehow-discordant chime sounded nothing like her own demented hammering: at least her hammering had sounded human.

And to be fair, at that point it had been hammer on the door like a hungry fool or else run screaming from the building, because everything about this place, from the polished concrete floor in the hallway that gleamed just a little off kilter, to the eerie light that came, as expected, from the roof but seemed to do so without any discernible source whatsoever, to that slight cloy in the air that vaguely called to mind rot without ever actually managing to smell like it... All of it had her vulturing her shoulders and darting glances around like her subconscious expected something to melt out of the walls and ensnare her.

Which, again to be fair, Not-A-Man literally had just appeared in thin air, so perhaps her subconscious knew what it was about.

Still. There was the trap to think about.

She hadn't really wanted Tristan to teach her his trick, of course, that was both pretence and foolishness.

She did need to stand on his rug, though—it was the only furnishing in the soulless room soft enough for what she needed—and she hadn't been able to think of anything else to say. It turned out that thirteen years was too long a conversational gap to surmount.

So she waited now as Tristan let the Not-A-Man in, closing the door behind him without even a glance down the corridor. Cool air wafted past, the ghost of the air in the apartment.

Nicole waited.

Somewhere outside something faint broke the silence, probably a crow cawing somewhere way down below at the foot of the building.

Which, that was a long way down. The building was huge, some thirty or so storeys high, and as far as she could make out, the only occupant was Tristan, the only useable space the penthouse; the other floors had stretched out blank and empty as she'd peeked into them from the stairwell windows, puffing and sweating because she hadn't trusted the idea of a lift with only a single destination: it could go to the penthouse floor, or the ground floor, and nothing in between.

Why have a building this huge only to house one prisoner?

Presumed prisoner. Nicole very much hoped that there was some sort of personal magical security that kept him here, because she'd certainly encountered nothing to stop her on her way in, and if he could have just waltzed out of here at any moment this entire time... She ground her teeth and shoved the wolf called Fury down.

A loud thud sounded behind the closed apartment door and Nicole tensed.

One.

Two.

Three.

Four.

The door burst open and Tristan peered wildly about. "Nicole?" he called. "Nicole? What did you do?"

He didn't know she was still there; he couldn't.

She pressed her back hard against the wall, heart hammering in her chest. "What I had to," she whispered. Her face crumpled against her father's shouts.

Long, slow breaths. One... Two... Three... Four...

Tristan withdrew, slamming his front door.

Nicole melted against the wall.

It was done.

TRISTAN LEANED HIS BACK AGAINST HIS FRONT DOOR and stared at the crumpled mess on the rug. The Not-A-Man's limbs splayed akimbo, his hair a tangled mess over skin now blistered and blue-grey.

The points of his ears had melted.

Even now, his body was shimmering with that same faint, silver light he'd always seemed to emanate, only this time the light was stronger, brighter—and it was beginning to overtake him until he faded clean away.

Nicole had done something. She had to have.

Panic squeezed its tight fist in Tristan's chest. He pressed his fingertips against the door behind him until they blanched.

What had she done?

She'd said she wasn't there to rescue him, so what was this? If not a rescue attempt, then what? Revenge?

He sagged, head bowing, scrabbling for sense and logic like a carp flapping madly in search of water.

Why? What did she want? This didn't serve her in learning his trick, and there was no point to it if she really had meant to free him because there were plenty more like the not-a-man who'd just disintegrated on Tristan's rug, an endless, uncountable supply of beings both human and not who were just as happy to enforce the conditions of Tristan's servitude, to collect payment from him, to make sure that—apart from four minutes a day—he stayed miserable enough to need them.

Tristan ran a hand over his head, fingers tangling in his dark hair.

The rug was clear, as red and empty as ever, only the faint traces of footprints indicating that anyone had ever stood there.

He crossed it, went to the window, sat down.

A raven tapped on the window, wings flaring to hold itself steady while it staccatoed a rhythm on the glass.

Tristan blinked. What in the world...?

The main windows didn't open—a sensible choice for the thirty-third floor of a building designed to house reluctant prisoners—but the short pane above the main window did, winding out a few inches or more to let in a bit of breeze. Tristan had stood on the bench seat and opened them once, early on, when he was still cataloguing the apartment in an attempt to maintain his sanity.

Then, just like now, they glided out silently as secrets, inching out to intrude into something that felt eerily akin to an abyss, even if he *could* see the ground way down below.

The raven performed a complicated bit of flight that led to it landing on the rim of the open window. "Caw," it said.

"Hello," said Tristan. "Can I help you?"

OUT IN THE HALLWAY, NICOLE COCKED HER HEAD. WAS that... a crow? Cawing? Cawing from *inside* the apartment? Her brow furrowed deeply.

THE RAVEN GAVE A GREAT FLAP OF WINGS. TRISTAN jumped back, which led to him landing heavily—poorly—on the tiled floor, one ankle rolling—and the raven landed on the wooden ladder-backed chair that always hovered by the square dining table.

The raven pecked at the wooden surface of the table—a grey sort of wooden, silvered as though with age.

Hungry, maybe, Tristan decided, so he limped his way to the kitchen, yanked a grey cupboard door open, and stared at the rows of cans and boxes blankly. What did ravens eat?

...Carrion, mostly, if he remembered correctly. At least, that was what he'd *seen* them eat.

He closed the cupboard door and opened the silver fridge instead. A teaspoon of leftover mince, rolled stickily between forefinger and thumb as he shut the cold air back away in the fridge and returned to the crow.

He held out the mince on his hand, fingers splayed widely so the bird wouldn't peck them— Or was that how you fed horses? He couldn't quite remember.

Never mind, didn't matter; the raven jumped, flipping its grip on the chair around so its feet faced Tristan, gave a happy sort of caw, and pecked up the delicious morsel.

Tristan blinked.

There was a raven in his apartment. His thirty-third floor apartment. His thirty-third floor apartment he'd lived in for thirteen years with never a visitor except for the...

His gaze shied away from the red rug.

"I would have liked a visit from you sooner," he murmured to the raven, imagining befriending it years back, the raven bringing him trinkets that reminded him of the outside world, he in turn providing it with food, and maybe even shelter.

He daydreamed, very briefly, about what life would have been like with the raven as a roommate.

Of course, for the raven, that would have been very much like what Tristan's life was now: providing trinkets and shiny pretties for someone who in turn supplied your food, your water, your shelter.

Oh sure, Tristan was technically free to go, just as the raven would have been. Except…

He tilted his head.

If the raven had gone—even if it had come and gone periodically—it would have done so because it wanted to, and for no other reason.

Well. Tristan's jaw jutted. He stayed because he wanted to. For Nicole's sake. For her safety. And for his. And for the safety of the world.

He glanced out the window, mostly at sky, dimming rapidly now from dusk to twilight.

A few stars were out.

His chest constricted. The stars burned bright, but no one sought to capture *them*.

The bird could bring trinkets all it liked, and no one would seek to cage it. Or, well, very few people would, anyway, and someone else would probably inform on them to the animal rights people.

A knock sounded at the door.

Tristan stared at the raven. "What," he murmured, "have I done?"

Despite her best efforts, Nicole's shoulders kept rising, tension tweaking the strings of them ever higher, and she knocked on the door with her heart in her throat. A crow? All she could see was the not-a-man transforming, shifting into something dark and feathered and winged—cawing loudly before stabbing out the eyes of the man she did—despite her best efforts—think of as her father.

The door swung open under her fist.

Tristan's face shifted through a cascade of emotions; he'd evidently been as concerned about what was going on outside the door as she was about what was going on inside.

"Are you—" she said, and stopped, because obviously he hadn't had his eyes pecked out and obviously he was okay and obviously he also was not, because if everything had gone according to plan, she'd just used all the breath of the not-a-man she'd been stealing every time he'd exhaled gold into her fishbowl to trap him and, with any luck, murder him.

She winced, not having ever described it quite so bluntly, even in the private confines of her mind.

"Are *you*...?" Tristan said, eyebrows rising.

Nicole nodded curtly. "I heard... a noise."

Tristan draped himself lethargically against the door, eyeing her through narrowed, slitted eyelids.

"I suppose you did," he said. "What if I'm distressed by it?"

Her jaw twitched, once, twice, a third time. "I suppose anyone might be distressed by the sudden appearance of a crow in one's apartment."

It was the right thing to say: he laughed.

"You'd better come in," he said. "I'm not sure how quickly they'll send out a replacement, or someone to investigate, or whatever..." A brief shake of his head. "But you don't want to be on the doorstep when they do."

She hadn't thought of that.

Her chest constricted as Tristan shut the door behind her, and she surveyed the vermillion rug, trying her level best to keep emotions away from her face.

"Hey," Tristan said, and lightly tapped the back of her hand, which had curled itself without her permission into a fist—he had used to do that when she was a child, she remembered, a quick triplicate as shorthand for *I love you*—"it's going to be okay."

She shivered.

Then, "Of course it's going to be okay," she snapped. "I got rid of *him*, didn't I?" She gestured to the empty rug. "Where is he now?" The kitchen was empty, and so was the window seat—

Ah, the crow was perching on the lampstand over near a doorway she presumed led to Tristan's bedroom.

Nicole narrowed her eyes at the bird.

"Oh, don't mind him," Tristan said, also eyeing up the crow. "He's just visiting. The, uh…" He stared down at the empty rug, expression thoughtful. "Well, *he* just sort of… vanished. In a sparkle of light. Silver," he said, meeting Nicole's eye, "if that matters."

She pursed her lips. Vanished? That hadn't been in the plan.

"What exactly did you do?" Tristan said with an air of professional curiosity. "If you don't mind my asking."

"You weave gold from sunlight," she said. "I"— she tossed her dark hair over her shoulder— "weave breath into… well, anything I like, really. I've been collecting *his* breath for years. That's the only problem with my, uh, trick. Breath takes even longer than gold to transmute into something valuable."

For reasons unknown, her heart began to pound.

Tristan stared at her—through her?—then blinked, slow and deliberate, like a lizard. "Why do you want to learn my trick then?" *Surely you have enough trouble of your own,* he clearly didn't add.

Nicole shrugged, her neck prickling, her scalp suddenly itchy. "I, um. This is the…" The rug just in front of her had a lush, thick pile to it, nice and insulating, trapped air well.

Tristan was still looking at her with his dark, sad eyes.

She shrugged and-or rolled her shoulders again. "I didn't really want yours. And I can't do it with everyone's breath," she added in a rush, because suddenly the idea of him misunderstanding her was more than she could bear, worse even than a decade plus without a father. "Only the... them. And my own. I just..." Never realised what other people meant when they said they could see their breath in the cold. I always see it. Didn't realise how different I really was. "I just needed to stand on your rug."

"My rug?" His eyebrows shot up.

The crow cawed from the lampstand, wings flapping as it shifted its balance.

"Well," she continued, face flushing hot, "I didn't know there would be a rug specifically. I just... needed somewhere to complete the trap. Something that would... hold the air." She waved, a non-specific gesture at the floor, helpless as she tried to explain something she could barely articulate even to herself.

What she meant was that, after five years of watching the not-a-man breathe gold from his hand into her fishbowl, she'd finally realised what it meant that she could see his breath swirling and pirouetting out from his mouth, and after two years of watching *that* she realised she could rig something to collect it all, and another two years after *that* she realised that she could do things with the breath she'd collected—and so she began collecting her own, and experimenting with it to see what could happen, and somehow she'd just *known* that what you did to the breath mirrored what you did to the body, and what you did to the body you did to the mind, and somehow the breath was the link between the two and she wasn't really sure how or why, but when she changed where she put her own breath, she changed how she felt— and sometimes, who she was.

"You meant to... to kill him?"

She looked sharply at Tristan, pulled from the anxious unspooling of her thoughts wherein she was seeing her own apartment, with its white walls and green trailing pot plants and that square of sunshine tracking down the wall and the hearts- ease, which was her favourite place to stash her breath, resting between its tiny serrated leaves... But Tristan's expression was frank enough, and she exhaled. "Yes. Or hoped to, anyway." She lifted her chin. "I'm not sad it worked."

"No." Tristan stared wistfully at the rug.

The crow cawed again, and flapped across the room to land on Tristan's arm, which he held out idly for it, preoccupied, a movement that looked like he had done it a thousand times.

Something tugged in Nicole's chest. What if she had been the crow? What if she had been the one flocking to his side, and he'd held out his arm just as easily, just as naturally for her, because he'd been a father, a real, actual, present father, hugging her like that for thirteen years?

"They'll send a replacement along presently,

though. You didn't rescue me, you know," he added, meeting her eyes with a sudden intensity.

She shrugged, and this time it was with practiced nonchalance, a movement that fitted her like a well-tailored coat. "I told you I wasn't here to."

She ignored the slithering sensation of regret in her stomach.

She hadn't come intending to rescue him. She was here for the other r-word—revenge—and that alone.

Really.

Tristan cocked his head.

The black bird—which, now Nicole looked at it, had a kind of oily, rainbow, iridescent sheen to its wings—leaned up to nibble gently at Tristan's ear.

He glanced at it, as though it had said something poignant, or at the very least pertinent, and he was pleased by this.

"So he's gone then?" Nicole said more loudly than she'd intended, working hard not to scowl at the bird.

"Hmm? Oh, yes. Vanished. Silver sparkles. I did say," Tristan added. "Look, you'd better go before the next one gets here. Not that I don't appreciate what you did," he added again, softening as she tensed, her shoulders vulturing. "It's just that... well... I guess I mean it doesn't really make much difference in the end." His eyes pleaded with her to understand.

Her fingers rolled into fists at her sides.

She understood. "Fine. Well. I said I wasn't here to rescue you, and I can see you're happy enough, what with your gold and your... friends." Okay so now she *was* scowling at the bird, but could anyone blame her? Her nails bit at her palms. "I don't particularly care what *you* do," she said. "But I don't need your help any more. No more gold. Don't send them around. I don't want anything to do with them." Or *you*. Her eyes prickled hot; her hands clenched, and so did her jaw. "I'm going now."

He tilted his head again, and the bird mimicked him. "What *I* do?"

Anger wrapped burning fingers around her throat. "Well I didn't come to rescue you, but I hoped... I meant... Urgh." She wheeled around, yanked the door open—and jumped.

It was sometimes hard to tell, of course, but facing her, one finger upraised as though to ring the bell, dark hair flowing to the shoulders over a leaf-green top that could have been a long tunic or a short dress, was probably a not-a-woman.

Nicole's pulse hammered. She scowled. "I'm just leaving," she said.

The not-a-woman's eyebrows lifted—but she stepped just slightly aside as Nicole, buoyed by anger and fuelled up on recklessness, pushed her way past into the hall, every hair on her body on end as though electrified by the possibility that the not-a-woman might try to stop her.

She didn't.

Nicole stormed down the hall to the stairwell.

Fine.

If he wanted to stay there and breathe sunlight into gold for people who were clearly exploiting him, if he was happy with his crows and his elf friends... *Not*, she thought as she ripped the heavy stairwell door open and warm, concrete-scented air came flooding up, that she had *expected* him to be happy, necessarily, when the not-a-man was murdered.

What *had* she expected?

Nothing.

Something else.

Not this.

She pounded down the concrete stairs, blood thundering in her ears.

Fine.

Let him stay here in his tower house and rot.

TRISTAN STARED FOR A LONG TIME AT THE EMPTY SPACE left by Nicole's departure.

The not-a... woman, he supposed... cleared her throat.

Her eyebrows were still raised, but now they were raised at *him*.

A shudder ran down him.

The raven gripped his arm tightly in its claws,

and he winced.

"Aelfweard has not returned," the not-a-woman said, and although there was no question to her tone, Tristan had to fight the urge to take a step back as she stepped in and shut the door behind her.

She eyed the rug narrowly, nostrils flaring, the faint, silvery non-light she too emanated pulsing as though she was seeing—or at least inferring—what had recently happened there.

What had Nicole hoped?

She'd said twice she wasn't there to save him.

But she'd hoped…?

The raven shifted, claws digging in again.

The not-a-woman sighed at the rug. "I would have liked to see him before… But"—her wistful tone became brusque and businesslike—"that is not a conversation for you. I see that you did not have a hand in what happened, so you have earned yourself a reprieve from the punishment I would otherwise have been compelled to offer. You could have intervened, however," she added sternly, eyebrows drawing down until two little vertical lines appeared above their inner edges. Her lips pursed tightly.

Tristan shifted under her scrutiny, and the raven gave another little flap.

"No," she said. "I suppose you could not have." She sniffed. "Well. What's done is done. Where is it, then?"

"I… I gave it to him." Tristan's heart raced, and

he swallowed down the urge to back away—which would have done no good anyway, his back being toward the window and the window being only a couple of paces behind.

He had, though, he'd given it to him, and the not-a-man with the curved and pointed ears had been crossing the rug to leave when... when it had happened, whatever it was Nicole had done with... Had she said she'd... stolen his breath, somehow? Or something?

He was wringing his hands.

The raven pecked at his ear, and it hurt, but only a little.

He stopped.

The not-a-woman's jaw was working. "No," she said. "You could not have, or it would have been left behind." She stooped, ran a hand over the vermillion rug, her fingers slithering between the thick pile. She rubbed her fingertips together. "See?" she said. "Nothing."

"I... I..." The window bench caught the back of Tristan's knees and he sat heavily.

The raven cawed disapprovingly and flapped over to the ladderback of the dining chair.

The temperature in the room hadn't changed—it couldn't, or at least not via any mechanism Tristan had been able to discover—but he was sweating regardless.

Nicole had hoped he would choose to leave.

After all, nothing was trapping him here.

Nothing except for this, the not-a-woman bearing slowly down on him, slinking toward him with hips that rolled beneath her short tunic and seemed to cry out for hands to grip them tight, her light eyes narrowed and focused with a determination that had his heart racing again in anticipation, and her dark hair shifted and the wicked, curved points of her ears were visible, and he wanted to run his thumb over them because even after all this time, the beauty that had drawn him to seek help in the forest still existed, and he swallowed hard with the cold, cold window pressed against his back and night falling in the forest outside the tower—

"I—" He swallowed again. "I want to leave."

She halted abruptly on the close edge of the vermillion rug. Her lips became a lascivious curve. "But what about your daughter?"

No more. I don't want any more gold from you. Not like that.

It wasn't precisely what she'd said, but something close enough. A shiver gripped him.

"I want to leave."

He pressed his eyes closed against the words that seemed to hang in the purified air of the room.

The raven cawed.

He heard the rustle of feathers, of wings—and the raven landed in his lap.

Tristan's eyebrows rose of their own accord.

The bird pecked gently at his chin.

He offered it his forearm, and once it had shifted and caught its balance, he stood. "I'm leaving now."

Abruptly she was in his face without seeming to have crossed the intervening distance. "But Tristan," she hissed. "Think of all the things we saved you from."

He stumbled as memories forcibly exploded in his mind:

The first friends who'd changed, knocking on his door late in the dark of night when the world lay silent and smelled of dew-damp grass, their furtive glances as they asked for 'just a little help'; the first time someone had pounded on his door, shaking the walls of the house, demanding he come out and 'use his talent for good', by which of course they meant pay off their gambling debt.

He'd tried to keep it secret as long as he could, after that first moment... Yep, there it was, that day near the end of high school when he'd shown his girlfriend what he could do, and she'd told her friends, and they'd told his friends, and before he'd known it he'd been standing on the outdoor basketball court surrounded by mutterings and whispers, and any walk across campus was filled with sidelong glances and furtive looks, and his best friend had stopped sitting with him in class because, "You should've told me, mate", which spiralled into snide remarks from the back row whenever the teacher called on Tristan, whenever Tristan didn't know the answer, whenever Tristan stumbled or fumbled or was human, because suddenly, this power, this talent, this *trick* that he had meant that he was supposed to be *more* than human, because no one else could stomach that maybe just a regular mortal had woken up one day with the ability to breathe sunlight into gold and if he had that talent then how *dare* he complain about *anything* else, because he was *blessed*, he was *blessed*, he was *blessed*.

Blessed people didn't make mistakes.

Blessed people didn't stuff up.

Blessed people were obligated to use their blessings for the Greater Good of anyone who could find them—and eventually everyone did, and Tristan shuddered from head to toe as the memory of the first time he'd been kidnapped engulfed him, petrol and hot oil and something musty in the boot of a car he'd been shoved head-first into, the pain searing down the side of his temple from where he'd sliced it on… something… and the taste of blood in the back of his throat and the bruises and knocks that caught with every bump in the road as his assailants transported him…

Tristan gasped in air, snatching for it, clinging to it.

He was not in the car.

His heart was pounding like it was, adrenalin electric in his veins.

He was not in the car.

The raven cawed softly.

"I don't… need… your protection… anymore."

He wrenched his eyes open.

The not-a-woman was a mere breath from his face, colours swirling iridescently over the surface of her eyes, and his foot had gone dead and numb and sweat was trickling down his temples and his mouth tasted rotten, spoiled adrenalin, festering fear, sour and manipulative and sickening.

She ran a soft finger down his check, wiping away the sweat.

It glistened on her fingertip.

She licked it away.

Gently—so, so gently, the raven still balanced on his other forearm—he nudged the not-a-woman back.

Once, he would have touched her ears as he left.

Once, he would have needed to.

But it wasn't closure he was after this time.

Something soared in his chest, fierce and enboldening. He had no word to name it—it had been a long, long time, time spent curating his emotions, cultivating his memories, pruning them until all he had was numbness and four minutes of happiness a day—but it flapped its wings, and he realised starlight was only sunlight from really far away.

Through the tint of the window behind him, he tugged on the sky with all his might.

He'd never done that before, never let himself go to see what he could really do.

Someone might have gotten hurt.

The stars answered him, filling him with light, with warmth... And he turned to the window and exhaled, and gold covered the window until the weight of it shattered the glass, and the night air rushed in, fierce and cold, lake-water and decomposing oak leaves, autumn and rain-smell all.

And Tristan pulled on the stars again, the raven's claws wound tightly around his arm, and they filled him up and he exhaled, and there in front of him, suspended in the air, the most magnificent gleaming chariot, intricate gold lattice-work like lace or snowflakes writ large, and he threw himself at it as the not-a-woman shrieked behind him—something something *protect you* something something *need us*—and the raven cawed and took flight, wheeling in great circles around the chariot breathed from sunshine and borne up by starlight.

It hadn't been that long; Nicole would still be in the forest somewhere.

If Tristan hurried, he could find her. Give her a ride home.

And then...

Well.

What happened then, no one knew, but for now he was skimming over the crystalline surface of the lake with the taste of it kissing his face, and the high-rise was diminishing into the distance behind him; to the casual observer, it might have even been nothing more than a strange, overly tall tree, or a mountain rising out of the woods, nothing spectacular, just the middle of nowhere.

Ravens cawed, and with feathered rustling circled around Tristan on his golden chariot as he left the lake behind, and the scent of leaf mould overtook him, autumn-gold leaves rustling in the starlight.

Exactly the right sort of clouds punctuated the sky, tiny wisps of fluff that lent contrast to the vastness of the stars, reminded the viewer that space was large and the Earth was small, and that even the largest and most magnificent of gestures was only that: a gesture.

Ahead, somewhere in the forest, a girl laughed.

Nicole.

That soaring, fierce sensation spread in Tristan's chest again.

He didn't know what he was.

No one cared.

And it was grand.

About The Author

AMY LAURENS is an Australian author of fantasy and science fiction for all ages. Her fantasy novella *Bones Of The Sea*, about creepy magical bones and carnivorous mist, won the 2021 Aurealis Award for Best Fantasy Novella.

Amy has also written the award-winning portal-fantasy *Sanctuary* series about Edge, a 13-year-old girl forced to move to a small country town because of witness protection (the first book is *Where Shadows Rise*), the humorous fantasy *Kaditeos* series, following newly graduated Evil Overlord Mercury as she attempts to acquire a castle, the young adult series *Storm Foxes*, about love and magic and family in small town Australia, and a whole host of shorter works.

Amy also writes non-fiction books, often on various aspects of writing. Also dogs. Lots of dogs.

You can find out more about her at
www.AmyLaurens.com

Read more by Amy Laurens!

Six fantasy short stories
available in print and ebook
from InkprintPress.com
and all major online retailers

AND THEN I SHALL TRANSFORM:

In Which Leaves Are Common Sense

Most people think leaves fall in autumn because they die, fluttering drifts of red and yellow and orange and brown, twirling on a breeze that smells like the promise of ice before falling to skitter along the ground with a hollow tick-tick-tick.

Most people, it turns out, are wrong.

About many things of course, but in this case about the leaves: deciduous trees don't just shed their leaves wantonly, carelessly—or even regretfully.

No.

Deciduous trees lose their leaves because they are frugal.

Turns out, the only reason the leaves change colour in the first place—be that ruby or pumpkin, butternut or hazel, or some striated rainbow in between—is because the cooling weather lulls the plant into sleepiness, and a sleeping plant is a plant that can't eat (frozen leaves aren't much good at collecting sunlight anyway, not when frost bursts their cell walls like bubbles, sharp fragments of ice severing pathways like a knife through warm, fresh neurons).

The colour change is just the outward signal of the tree's common sense: drawing back in all the nutrients the leaf has to offer, slurping them back into the trunk where the tree can nurse on them all winter long, shedding the now-empty leaves like scales, sloughing them off like old skin, discarding dead storage units until the risk of frostbite has passed.

The day I realised I could do the same changed my life.

The snow was—predictably—cold. It was also early, and I'd been caught out hiking unprepared, which was just about the dumbest thing I'd managed to do yet in my life—apart from, maybe, George, and also attending New Beat University. An avid hiker since I'd been old enough to carry any sort of day pack with my parents, I knew the risks inside and out, backward and forward, upside and down.

Never go hiking alone.

Always pack extra Puritabs.

Let people know where you're going, and when you expect to be back.

Take warmer things than you think you'll need.

No one gives advice on what to do when your hike-mate has a sudden attack of lunar-cy, though, three days before the full moon. No one tells you what to do when you're abruptly alone in a sea of grey-trunked eucalypt trees and tea tree scrub that stinks like face cleanser and scratches like the blazes, and you've now got two packs' worth of gear to hike out. Alone.

Werewolves are not considerate hiking buddies, let me be the first to assure you.

Well. Amendment: Probably some of them are, maybe even most of them.

George? Not so much.

(In hindsight, unsurprising: he'd never been a very considerate roommate, either, no matter what physical form he was in.)

And, of course, it was cold.

And as I stood in the clearing where considerate wildlife had trampled down the tussock grass and a fallen gum tree was busy turning silver as it weathered, cold air singeing the inside of my nostrils and burning the tip of my nose, I realised I had a choice: I could get really, *really* cold as I sat around waiting for George to human up again—probably in three or four days once the moon had passed, but then again, he wasn't supposed to have wolfed out this earlier either, so who knew?—or I could get really really warm trying to hike two packs' worth of gear back out.

Or—I scratched my nose, face screwed up—I could redistribute the gear, take the expensive or vital stuff out in one pack, leave the rest somewhere covered and come back when it was safe.

With someone other than George, of course.

Bloody George.

I sighed heavily, rolled my pack over onto its back like a floundering sea lion, and began unbuckling the straps. Stupid to think I could hike a whole day out with both full packs. Not worth the risk.

The sky told me what it thought of that: the clouds that had been fitfully scudding across the sky coagulated into something thick and soupy and so low it seemed like I could practically touch it (or at least throw something high enough to touch it, like a rock, or maybe George, who deserved to be tossed into the sky) and the sky began to spit at me.

I rolled my eyes at the melodrama, rustled the brim of my cherry-red raincoat down over my forehead, and set about repacking the packs.

Out came my bag of dirty clothes. Would I regret leaving them if I needed extra warmth? Probably not.

Stupid weather, sky-spit freezing my fingers and making them slow.

Sleeping mat. Ditched. I had one night max to spend outdoors, and that was if I spent the rest of today lollygagging around instead of moving at pace.

Stupid moon, exerting whatever stupid influence it was over stupid werewolves at a stupid time of the month.

Sleeping bag.

Well. Obviously I was going to hold onto that one, just in case.

Only one though. George could keep his own furry butt warm if it came to that.

Food—check, definitely coming with. Compass, maps, cook stove—yes, yes and yes.

Tent. Obviously. Just in case.

Dammit. I'd have to take both halves.

I fished the fly and poles out of George's pack and rammed them into my own.

The sky stopped spitting and started snowing at me, frigid air turning my fingers red, the scent of the bush subtly shifting from eucalypt to wet grass and now to snow itself.

The hell.

It was March. Yes, okay, fine, it was autumn by the calendar, but the last five, ten years March had grown *hot*. Like, summer hot. No one reasonably expected even a sudden transient fit of cold weather until April, which was why I'd agreed to this hike with George in the first place.

A cold snap? Sure. Unfortunate, but this wasn't our first hike in the bush and we'd brought layers.

Snow?

What. The actual. Hell.

I scowled at the steely clouds, shoved the last of the necessities into my pack, and drew the drawstring tight around its neck.

Flipped the lid of the pack shut, canvas scuffing loudly in the silence of the bush. Snapped the buckles shut—snap, snap, echoing around the clearing.

A third snap.

I froze.

My pack definitely only had two buckles to close, and George's pack was right there in front of me, wallowing on the ground like an unholy grey hippopotamus.

My ears tried to crawl off my head as I tried to surveil the bush around me without appearing to.

...A rustle, perhaps? Behind and to my left, where the gum trees thinned in both density and girth and the spiky, pale tussock grass traced a path down a gentle slope to a green hollow largely occupied by a white cedar of impressive height.

The dang berries on the cedar were toxic. I knew that. George knew that. But did George's lunar form know that?

I may or may not have let my pack fall sideways with a bit of firm assistance as I swore and clambered to my feet.

Definitely a rustle, that now became a susurrus of disturbed grass as something grey and the size of a large kangaroo or a small wolf vanished into the teatree scrub.

I ground my teeth. Inhaled icy-cold air. Buried my hands under my armpits and cursed past-me momentarily for not packing gloves, summer-like weather be damned. Then I trudged after the critter toward the hollow.

The white cedar gleamed like a golden crown amid the grey-and-olive eucalypts, framed above by the grey sky, its buttery autumn leaves flipping and fluttering in a breeze no other tree seemed to feel.

And underneath it, George: a grey wolf resting on his haunches with a wide, doggy grin on his face, tongue lolling to one side.

"George," I said sternly, "I have too far to hike today to be messing around anymore with you. Either get your butt back here and let me strap a pack to your furry hide, or leave me alone so I can get home without losing my fingers to frostbite."

I burrowed my hands deeper into my armpits, which probably would have been more effective if I'd had them under my raincoat, but that would mean opening said raincoat, which, no.

As if sensing the nearness of the end of my emotional tether, the sky very kindly hit pause on the whole snow situation.

My nose still burned with the cold.

"On second thoughts, get your furry butt over here so I can bury my face in it for a moment and warm up." My nose wrinkled. "Your fur, that is, I'm not burying my face in your butt."

George's grin didn't budge. He'd told me before that he had a hard time remembering how language worked while he was a wolf, but I squinted at him nonetheless.

"If you laugh, I'll murder you on the spot."

Happy panting.

Heaving a sigh to end all sighs, rolling my eyes hard enough that even Temporary Wolf Boy couldn't fail to read my emotions, I stomped back to the clearing where I'd left the packs.

The packs were gone.

For the splittiest of seconds, I froze again—and then because I was actually starting to freeze, I strode to the spot where the packs had lain, thin rapiers of grass still crushed and buckled in their wake, and howled, "George!!"

To his credit, he appeared almost instantly at the fringe of the clearing again, peering out between the gnarled and twisted fingers of the tea tree.

"Where," I said, "are our packs?" As if staring at him sternly with my hands on my hips would suddenly spur him to speech.

I ground my teeth.

The clouds hung above, not even a little movement in them to indicate the passing of time, no glimpse of the sunlight we'd been expecting shining through. Surely it was at least mid-morning now though, and I had, what, six hours to hike out to safety?

Fine.

Fine, I'd do it without George, without the packs—and without water I realised with a sinking stomach.

Okay.

Okay fine.

That would suck, but it was six hours, maybe seven or eight if I took it really slow to conserve energy, and sunset wasn't until... I narrowed my eyes. *I don't know, maybe five thirty, six o'clock? It was twilight when I was sitting down to dinner on Tuesday and that was...*

Sure, sunset was maybe six o'clock if I was lucky.

So I had six, maybe eight hours to walk on six, maybe seven, possibly eight hours of daylight.

Easy.

Absolutely plausible.

And it was freezing, so no doubt I'd drink less anyway. Ah ha. Ah ha-ha ha ha.

At least I'd walk faster without a pack.

Keep reading! Head to
inkprintpress.com/amylaurens/
shalltransform/
to buy your copy now!